Scholastic, the #1 most trusted name in learning, brings you Dora, Little Bill, Blue and reading adventures too!

When kids watch their favorite Nick Jr. characters on TV, each top-rated show encourages them to play to learn – from finding clues or following a map, to using their imaginations.

Now, Nick Jr. books take your child on more playful adventures that reinforce early learning skills. Each exclusive story introduces a different lesson on colors and shapes, science and nature, math, reading, problem-solving ... even how to handle emotions.

You won't find these hardcover books in any store. They're only available from Scholastic, the #1 name in children's publishing. Let Scholastic's *Nick Jr. Book Club* turn story time into play time at your home and keep your child laughing and learning.

Send now for
8 BOOKS
FOR JUST $3.99*
Plus 3 FREE GIFTS!

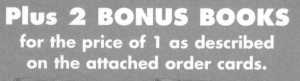

FREE

FREE

FREE

NICK JR BOOK CLUB

Play Pages

Parents Guide

Magenta's Super Sleepover

Animal Parade

*Plus shipping, handling and applicable sales tax

SCHOLASTIC
www.homeclubs.scholastic.com

Dear Parent,

We want to send you these eight Nick Jr. storybooks to encourage your child's love of reading.

As the most trusted name in learning today, we know just what that takes! Scholastic's books have been used by thousands of teachers across the country to teach millions of children to read. We're the #1 resource for parents like you for the widest variety of innovative products that help their children learn at home.

Parents turn to us to find just the right products for their children's specific needs and interests. From programs to enrich their children's skills ... sensible solutions to pressing concerns ... homework help, research projects, reading tips and more.

After all, we're parents, too! And, speaking as a mom, these Nick Jr. books make story time one of the best times my family shares! My kids love the lively adventures of their favorite Nick Jr. friends. I love the way each interactive book gently introduces and reinforces important learning skills. Plus, they're short and simple enough for my children to "read" and feel the pride of instant success.

So, enjoy this book with your child right now. Then fill out and mail one of the order cards at left and watch your child start learning ... and loving every minute of it!

Sincerely,

Mary-Alice Moore
Editorial Director
(and mother of three!)

This book belongs to
my friend:

_____

A NOTE TO PARENTS

Dora's Nursery Rhyme Adventure features several classic nursery rhymes that most preschoolers know and enjoy repeating. Not only are nursery rhymes entertaining, but they also help familiarize children with the sounds and words that make up language. In this story, Dora and her little brother and sister sing nursery rhymes to help Jack and Jill, Humpty Dumpty, and Old King Cole get out of trouble.

When Dora begins a rhyme, invite your child to complete the rest of it before you reveal the rhyme's end. If your child is still learning her rhymes, read a few lines and then ask her to guess the next rhyming word. Ask your child how she thinks the rhyme might solve each tricky situation. Discuss which nursery rhyme characters your child would like to meet.

You can reinforce this story's problem-solving skills by asking your child what other items could have been helpful if they were in Dora's backpack. For instance, what would have helped Dora and her friends jump over the candlestick? Use the story's silliness to tap into your child's creativity. Encourage her to make up a new rhyming verse or alternative endings to the nursery rhymes—you can write down what your child says, and then she can illustrate.

Learning Fundamental: **problem solving**

For more parent and kid-friendly activities, go to www.nickjr.com.

Dora's Nursery Rhyme Adventure

ENGLISH/SPANISH GLOSSARY and PRONUNCIATION GUIDE

English	Spanish	Pronunciation
Where is	Dónde está	DOHN-day eh-STAH
Thank you	Gracias	GRAH-see-ahs
You're welcome	De nada	deh NAH-dah
Help me	Ayúdenme	ah-YOO-den-may
Jump	Salta	SAHL-tah
Good-bye	Adiós	ah-dee-OHS

Published by Scholastic Inc., 90 Old Sherman Turnpike, Danbury, CT 06816

SCHOLASTIC and associated logos are trademarks and/or registered trademarks of Scholastic Inc.

ISBN 0-7172-7794-1

Printed in the U.S.A.

First Scholastic Printing, September 2005

Dora's Nursery Rhyme Adventure

by
Christine Ricci

illustrated by
Jason Fruchter

SCHOLASTIC INC.

New York   Toronto   London   Auckland   Sydney
Mexico City   New Delhi   Hong Kong   Buenos Aires

One day, Dora was reading *The Big Book of Nursery Rhymes* to her baby brother and sister. The twins snuggled up next to their big sister to hear their favorite rhyme.

"*Jack and Jill went up the hill*
To fetch a pail of water . . ."

Suddenly, Dora and the babies saw a big rain cloud fly over Jack and Jill's hill, and a powerful storm began to blow.

The storm was so strong
that it blew Jack and Jill
down the hill!

After the cloud blew away and the storm had stopped, Dora and the twins noticed that Jack and Jill had tumbled far from their hill.

"Help!" cried Jack and Jill. "We've got to get back to our hill!"

"We need to use our story powers to help Jack and Jill," exclaimed Dora. "Are you ready for a storybook adventure?"

The babies nodded excitedly. Then Dora and the twins held hands and jumped into the book!

Dora and the twins landed right next to Jack and Jill.
"We can help you get back to your hill," said Dora.
"But our hill is very far away," Jack observed.
"And we don't know how to get there," said Jill.

"Who helps us when we don't know which way to go?" asked Dora.
"Map!" shouted the babies.

"I can tell you how to get to the hill," said Map. "First you have to go past Humpty Dumpty, then go past Old King Cole's Castle, and that's how you'll get to Jack and Jill's hill."

"So, first we have to find Humpty Dumpty," Dora said.
"*¿Dónde está?* Where is Humpty Dumpty?"
The babies spotted Humpty Dumpty in the distance.

"I'm lost," cried Humpty Dumpty when they reached him. "I got turned around during the storm, and now I don't know where I belong."

"We'll help you," said Dora. "Our story powers will tell us where you belong." She started to sing: "*Humpty Dumpty sat on a . . .*"

"Wall!" exclaimed the twins.

As Humpty Dumpty climbed to the top of his wall, the babies suddenly remembered the rest of the nursery rhyme:

"*Humpty Dumpty had a great fall;*
All the King's horses and all the King's men
Couldn't put Humpty together again!"

"Oh no!" cried Dora. "Humpty Dumpty might get hurt. Maybe Backpack has something to cushion his fall."

"Pillows!" suggested the babies.

The babies, Jack and Jill, and Dora made a soft landing spot next to the wall.

"*¡Gracias!*" said Humpty. "Now I'll be safe."

"*De nada,*" Dora replied. "Next, we have to find Old King Cole's Castle."

"I see the castle,"
called Humpty Dumpty.
"Just follow the green path."
"Thanks, Humpty!"
Jack and Jill called.

When Dora, Jack and Jill, and the babies arrived at Old King Cole's Castle, the door was open, so they peeked inside. Much to their surprise, the castle was a mess!

"Looks like the rain cloud came through here, too," observed Jack.

Just then they heard a cry coming from the next room. "*¡Ayúdenme!* Help me!"

"C'mon!" urged Dora. "It sounds like Old King Cole needs our help!"

Inside, they found the King. "I've lost everything that makes me merry," he sobbed.

"We need to figure out what makes him happy," Dora said. "How does that rhyme go?"

The babies started to sing:

"Old King Cole
Was a merry old soul,
And a merry old soul was he.
He called for his pipe,
He called for his bowl,
And he called for his fiddlers three."

"Great!" Dora exclaimed. "We need to find a pipe, a bowl, and three fiddlers."

Dora, the twins, and Jack and Jill found everything that made the King happy.

"Thanks for helping me," Old King Cole said merrily. "Now how can I help you?"

"Can you help us find our hill?" asked Jack and Jill.

The King took everyone to the top of the castle's highest tower.

"I see lots of hills," said Dora. "Which one is Jack and Jill's hill?"

"Our hill has a well on the top of it so we can fetch a pail of water," Jack told them.

"Ah, yes," said the King. "There is your hill."

As they continued down the path, a candlestick suddenly blocked the road.

"What should we do?" wondered Jill.

"Maybe the nursery rhyme can help us," said Dora.

"*Jack, be nimble; Jack, be quick; Jack, jump over the candlestick!*" the babies chimed in.

"The rhyme says that I should jump," said Jack.

"Let's all jump over the candlestick," Dora suggested.

"Jump!" shouted Jack and Jill.

"*¡Salta!*" yelled Dora and the babies.

Everyone jumped safely over the candlestick!

Finally Dora, the twins, and Jack and Jill
reached the hill and climbed to the very top.
Suddenly, the rain cloud appeared again.

"Oh, no!" cried Jack. "What are we going to do? We'll never fill our pail with water."

"Don't worry," said Dora. "We know what to do!" Dora and the babies started to sing: "*Rain, rain, go away; Come again another day.*"

"I don't like that nursery rhyme!" puffed the rain cloud, and he blew far, far away.

"Hooray!" everyone cheered.

Jack and Jill gave Dora and the babies a big hug.

After saying good-bye to Jack and Jill, Dora and the babies jumped out of *The Big Book of Nursery Rhymes* and landed back in the babies' room. Soon the babies were sound asleep.

"Well, that was quite a nursery rhyme adventure,"
Dora whispered as she kissed them goodnight.
'We did it!"

THE BIG BOOK OF
NURSERY
RHYMES